THE STORY OF
ROBIN HOOD
COLORING BOOK

JOHN GREEN

DOVER PUBLICATIONS, INC.
MINEOLA, NEW YORK

Bibliographical Note

The Story of Robin Hood Coloring Book is a new work, first
published by Dover Publications, Inc., in 2018.

International Standard Book Number

ISBN-13: 978-0-486-82802-2
ISBN-10: 0-486-82802-6

Manufactured in the United States by LSC Communications
82802601   2018
www.doverpublications.com

INTRODUCTION

The legend of Robin Hood dates back to at least the fourteenth century. While Robin Hood's origins lie in English ballads, there have been efforts to prove that Robin Hood was a real historical figure. Regardless of whether or not he existed, Robin Hood has touched and inspired many generations.

The story takes place in occupied England, where there is no peace. The country is divided and ruled under strict feudal laws by powerful Norman barons. The Saxons are treated as mere serfs and ruled with a "rod of iron."

King Richard I came to the throne in 1189, and he soon left England to join the Crusades in the Holy Land. King Richard instructed the Bishop of Ely to rule for him during his absence, but King Richard's brother, Prince John, accused the bishop of treason. Prince John was a merciless and greedy man. Most barons, knights, and bishops were in league with him and were greedy as well. Two such men were the Sheriff of Nottingham and Guy of Gisborne.

Under the yoke of the Normans, many Saxon yeomen were robbed of their homes and livelihoods. They were outlawed and lived in the forests. In the twelfth century, much of England was covered in forests and Sherwood Forest in Nottinghamshire was one of the largest. All forests were the property of the king, and the penalty for hunting deer was cruel and barbarous.

Enter Robin, who becomes a skilled archer, rebel against injustice, and hero of the people.

Nottingham Castle is surrounded by Sherwood Forest. The forest is full of
ancient trees and deer roaming freely.

Robin's father, the Earl of Loxley and a Saxon, teaches Robin archery.
Young Robin excels.

Robin meets the lovely Maid Marian Fitzwalter while traveling
through Nottingham town.

Robin and Maid Marian hunt together in Sherwood Forest.

In the absence of the true king, the tyrant Prince John is now the ruler of England. His brother, Richard the Lionheart, is imprisoned in Austria.

King John dispenses his henchman, Guy of Gisborne, to Nottingham
to help collect taxes.

6

Guy's arrival in Nottingham upsets the people.

Robin rescues Midge, an orphan who is caught unlawfully hunting deer for food.

The Sheriff of Nottingham and Guy plot together.

Guy and his men rob a landowner. Robin's father, the Earl of Loxley, tries to prevent it and is killed.

Guy attacks Loxley Hall because the Loxley family has rebelled
against Prince John.

Robin tries to defend his home but is outnumbered.

Robin escapes into Sherwood Forest, pursued by Guy and his men.

Robin has been outlawed. He vows to avenge the death of his father and protect the poor. He is now known as Robin Hood and has a band of followers.

Little John and Robin Hood challenge each other to cross the bridge.

15

Little John and Robin Hood fight on the bridge.

Robin Hood and his men attack the sheriff's men, who are collecting
taxes from the people.

Robin Hood meets a stranger dressed in scarlet in Sherwood Forest.
He is known as Will Scarlet.

Robin Hood mocks Will Scarlet's appearance. Will becomes annoyed
and draws his sword.

Later Robin and Will become good friends. They discover that they are cousins. They meet Allan-a-Dale, a sad minstrel who has been prevented from marrying her sweetheart.

On his way back to Sherwood Forest, Robin meets the jovial, portly Friar Tuck, who is eating a pie, drinking ale, and making merry. Friar Tuck invites Robin to join him.

Robin tricks Friar Tuck to carry him across the river.

Robin and his men make merry at their camp in Sherwood Forest.

Robin and Little John encounter a sorrowful knight. An evil bishop has imprisoned his son and seized his property.

Robin helps the knight rob the bishop.

The knight pays the bishop with the bishop's own money, stolen by Robin.
He clears his debt to release his son from prison and retrieve his property.

Robin pretends to be a butcher selling cheap beef to trick the
Sheriff of Nottingham.

The Sheriff of Nottingham tries to persuade the butcher to sell his whole
herd cheaply to make a huge profit.

The Sheriff of Nottingham is tricked by Robin. He pays Robin for
the king's own deer.

The angry Sheriff plans to set a trap for Robin. He organizes an archery competition, with a silver arrow as the prize.

Robin disguises himself as a beggar to take part in the competition.

Robin shoots his last arrow in the competition.

Robin wins the silver arrow, which is awarded by the sheriff's wife. The sheriff and Guy look on aghast, wondering how a one-eyed beggar could be so good at archery.

Robin sends the sheriff and Guy a message wrapped around an arrow.
It reads, "I have fooled you again." The sheriff is humiliated.

Robin is still in his beggar disguise. On his way to Sherwood Forest, he comes across a startled boy who draws a dagger.

Robin realizes that the boy is Marian. She dressed as a boy in order to seek
out Robin in Sherwood Forest.

The Sheriff and Guy become very angry. They are determined to capture
Robin and Marian. The two are surrounded by Guy's soldiers.

Out of nowhere comes a knight dressed in black and riding a black charger.

The Black Knight comes to Robin and Marian's rescue.

Guy pursues Robin, and they fight fiercely. Robin is victorious and kills Guy.

Robin questions "strangers" who are dressed as pilgrims and traveling
through the forest.

One stranger reveals himself to be King Richard. He had dressed as a pilgrim to avoid being recognized. King Richard pardons Robin and his men.

Robin and Marian get married in Sherwood Forest. The wedding is attended by King Richard and Robin's merry men.

As an old man, Robin shoots his last arrow. Little John is there with him, as is Will
Scarlet, who is distraught. Robin says, "Where the arrow falls, there bury me."